FROGGY'S LEMONADE STAND

FROGGY'S LEMONADE STAND

by JONATHAN LONDON

illustrated by FRANK REMKIEWICZ

VIKING

For Helene & Evie, Doran & Iris, Aaron,
Steph & Sean, Eli, Regina, and sweet Maureen
  —J.L.

For David and Jean Mitchell
  —F.R.

VIKING
Penguin Young Readers
An imprint of Penguin Random House LLC
375 Hudson Street
New York, New York 10014

First published in the United States of America by Viking, an imprint of Penguin Random House LLC, 2018

Text copyright © 2018 by Jonathan London
Illustrations copyright © 2018 by Frank Remkiewicz

LIBRARY OF CONGRESS CATALOGING-IN-PUBLICATION DATA
Names: London, Jonathan, date– author. | Remkiewicz, Frank, illustrator.
Title: Froggy's lemonade stand / by Jonathan London ; illustration, Frank Remkiewicz.
Description: First edition. | New York : Viking Books for Young Readers, [2018] | Series: Froggy | Summary: Although many things go wrong when
Froggy decides to make money by setting up a lemonade stand, he still has fun with his friends. |
Identifiers: LCCN 2017036442 (print) | LCCN 2017046355 (ebook) | ISBN
9781101999721 (ebook) | ISBN 9781101999677 (hardcover) | ISBN
9781101999684 (trade paperback)
Subjects: | CYAC: Lemonade—Fiction. | Moneymaking projects—Fiction. | Frogs—Fiction. | Humorous stories. | BISAC: JUVENILE FICTION / Animals /
Frogs & Toads. | JUVENILE FICTION / Concepts / Money. | JUVENILE FICTION / Humorous Stories.
Classification: LCC PZ7.L8432 (ebook) | LCC PZ7.L8432 Fvl 2018 (print) | DDC [E]—dc23
LC record available at https://lccn.loc.gov/2017036442

Manufactured in China   Set in ITC Kabel Std   These illustrations were made with watercolor.

10 9 8 7 6 5 4 3 2 1

It was hot.
Froggy woke up
and looked out the window.
The sun was shining like a gold coin!
Aha! he said to himself.
That gives me a great idea!

So he hopped out of bed
and got dressed—*zip! zoop! zup!*
zut! zut! zut! zat!—
and flopped to the kitchen
for breakfast—*flop flop flop.*

"Mom!" he said, jumping up on his chair.
"I'm going to have a lemonade stand,
and make lots and lots of money!"

"Good idea!" said his mother.
"But first, eat your breakfast, dear."

So Froggy ate his breakfast of cereal and flies—
munch crunch munch—
and thought about what he could buy
with all the money he made.

Let's see, he thought: A new hula hoop—
A new pogo stick—*boing! boing! boing!*
A new superhero cape—*zoom!*

Then he said, "Okay! Time to
sell some lemonade!" And he
jumped up and flopped outside—
flop flop flop.

FRROOGGYY!

called his mother.

"Wha-a-a-t?"

"First you have to make the lemonade, dear!"

"Oops!" cried Froggy. "I know that!"

And he picked some lemons
from their lemon tree . . .

then raced into the kitchen
and started squeezing them
into a pitcher, singing,
"Easy-peasy, lemon squeezy . . ."

"Ouch!" cried Froggy.
"I squirted lemon juice in my *eye!*"

When the pitcher was full, he poured in a whole box of sugar—*zloop!*— then lots and lots of ice cubes— *zplat! zplat! zplat!*

and then he stuck his finger in to taste it.

"Yum!" said Froggy.

And he flopped back outside with the lemonade—
flop flop flop—(and he only splashed half of it out).
"FFRROOGGYY!" called his mom.
"Wha-a-a-a-t?"
"You forgot to make a lemonade stand!"
"Oops! I know that!"

Now, with a little help from Mom and Dad,
Froggy made a lemonade stand—*bang! bang! bang!*
Then he hammered up a sign and shouted:
"FREE LEMONADE FOR SALE! Twenty-five cents!"

"But Froggy," said Mom.
"How could it be free if it costs
twenty-five cents?"
"Oops!" cried Froggy.
And he drew a line through the word
FREE—*zwish!*

Then he sat down, and waited
for his first customer to come.
He waited and waited and waited,
and it got hotter and hotter.

And every time Froggy got thirsty,
he drank a cup of lemonade—
glug glug glug!

And by the time his first customer,
Frogilina, came and said, "Hi, Froggy!
A cup of lemonade, please!"
just *two* drops dripped out of
the pitcher—*zplish! zplish!*
All the lemonade was gone!

"Oops!" said Froggy. And he ran off . . .

and raced back with an old soccer trophy.
"One soccer trophy for sale! Twenty-five cents!"
"But Froggy, what I *really* want is—"

Just then, Max showed up and said,
"Hi, Froggy! A cup of lemonade, please!"
Froggy ran off . . .

and rushed back with a busted saxophone.
"One saxophone for sale! Twenty-five cents!"
"But Froggy, what I *really* want is—"

Just then, Matthew showed up and said,
"Hi, Froggy! A cup of lemonade, please!"
"Yikes!" said Froggy.
And he jumped up, ran off . . .

and dashed back with
a broken baseball bat.
"One baseball bat for sale!
Twenty-five cents!"
"But Froggy, what I *really* want is . . ."

everybody shouted.
Even Pollywogilina.

"Oh, I give up!" cried Froggy. "Follow me!"
And he led everybody back into the kitchen.
"Oops!" said Froggy. "There's no sugar left!
And all the ice is melted!
And all the lemons are gone!"

"I'll help you pick some more!" said Frogilina.
"And I'll get some sugar!" said Max.
"And I'll get some ice!" said Matthew.
"Good idea!" said Froggy.

While Max and Matthew ran off, Frogilina climbed the lemon tree and picked lemons.

And when Max came back with a box
of sugar and Matthew came back
with a bucket of ice . . .
they all made lemonade together, singing:
"Easy-peasy, lemon squeezy!"

Then they ran outside and had a wild lemonade party around the lemonade stand.

FRROOGGYY!

called his dad.
"Wha-a-a-t?"
"So, how much money did you make?"

"Oops!" cried Froggy, looking
more red in the face than green.
"I didn't make *one* cent!"

"But—we all had a great time!"
"YES!" cried his friends.